RISE OF THE SUPERNOVA

BEFORE THE LEGEND, THERE WAS JUST A CHOICE

VICKY SONAWANE

To my family, for their endless support and love.
To my close ones, who always have my back.
And to every dreamer who dares to imagine
beyond the stars.

Contents

Preface

I first started dreaming of this world when I was in 9th standard, sitting in a classroom with a head full of wild ideas and a heart drawn to fiction, animation, and gaming. Back then, I didn't yet have the words — or the courage — to bring this story to paper. I wasn't mature enough to shape it the way I knew it deserved. But the spark was always there. Over the years, that spark grew. What once was just a dream became a vision I couldn't let go of. I started to see the story clearer, feel the emotions deeper, and understand what it really meant to create something that lives beyond yourself.

This book is a piece of that dream — a long-held hope that has finally come true. Writing this book changed me. There were moments I doubted myself, wanted to stop, and wondered if it even mattered. But the characters reminded me why I started. They carried pieces of people I've loved, moments I've lived, and dreams I never said out loud.

If you're holding this, thank you. Thank you for stepping into this story — for giving it life beyond my imagination. And now, it's all yours.

Foreword

I've known about Rise of Supernova way before it had a name, a cover, or even a first chapter. My friend came up with this story back in 9th grade — when most of us were just trying to survive math class, he was out here imagining galaxies and superpowered characters like it was no big deal.

Years passed, and life happened — college, chaos, all of it. But that idea? It stayed. And one day, he just said, "I'm finally gonna write that book." Honestly, I wasn't sure if he was serious at first. But two years, countless drafts, late-night writing marathons, and a bunch of roadblocks later — here we are.

He actually did it. He turned that teenage daydream into a full-blown sci-fi story. And not just any story — it's his story. Not because it's autobiographical (thankfully, he doesn't have superpowers... yet), but because it's full of his persistence, creativity, and that wild imagination he never let go of.

Why should you read this? Because it's not just about space or supernovas — it's about chasing something you believed in when no one was watching. And also, because it's a pretty damn cool read.

So yeah — welcome to Rise of Supernova. You're in for something special.

— Dipanshu Wanjari

Prologue

I have a question to you, what are we? Human being? yes we are, we are normal human being who wants to leave a peaceful human life, just like everyone wants too.

He was also expecting such a life which he deserve. but destiny has some other plans for him, something really unexpected and unimaginable for anyone..! His life was about to undergo a profound transformation, imagine being a young person and suddenly having the weight of whole world on your shoulders. yes, the entire world..!

Well, buckle up because this is the rollercoster journey of [characters name] and i am vicky, narrating this goosebump-inducing tale for you. Lets dive in from beginning.

Urban Symphony

As the sun peeked through the curtains, "**Alex**" woke up in his cozy row house. The sounds of the city waking up outside his window mixed with the smell of breakfast cooked by his mom. His mom, a constant pillar of support, was in the kitchen, joined by his younger sister who were giggling and setting the table.

As the sun played hide-and-seek with the morning curtains, Alex ambled into the kitchen of his row house, where the aroma of a hearty breakfast wafted through the air. His younger sister, always the early riser, was energetically narrating a dream that involved a talking unicorn, causing Alex to exchange amused glances with his mom. Amidst giggles, they couldn't help but wonder if the unicorn had offered any wise advice for the day. The breakfast table turned into a stage for quirky morning conversations, and just as Alex was savoring the last bite of his toast, a sudden realization hit him like a splash of cold water—he was getting late for college! With a quick grab of his books, a rushed 'good morning' to his family, and a promise to catch up later, he hurried out the door. The city outside was buzzing with life, and Alex knew he had a day full of college adventures waiting.

However, behind the college lies a looming presence—the mysterious mountain that casts an enigmatic shadow over the campus. Whispers of chilling horror stories surround this mountain, tales that have been passed down from one batch of students to another. The mountain becomes a constant backdrop, a mysterious force that both intrigues and unsettles the students.

As Alex and his best friend, "**Marc**", walked towards the college, the familiar city sounds formed a comforting backdrop. Engrossed in conversation, they discussed the upcoming lectures with a mix of excitement and dread. Marc, with a mischievous glint in his eye, couldn't resist poking fun at their chemistry teacher, recounting a moment when the teacher accidentally mixed up two harmless chemicals during an experiment, resulting in a small but amusing explosion of foam. The memory had Alex chuckling, and together, they shared lighthearted quips about the quirky incidents that made their college days memorable. The anticipation of lectures mingled with the joy of shared laughter as they approached the college gates, ready to face whatever the day had in store.

Between classes, Alex and Marc found a nice spot in the college courtyard to chill. The sunny benches became their meeting spot, surrounded by the buzz of students and city sounds. They started chatting casually, and the talk turned to the eternal question: 'Pineapple on Pizza.' Marc loved it, arguing for the sweet and savory mix, while Alex stuck to the classic margherita defense. Their banter turned into a bet—whoever lost treated the winner to lunch. The bell rang, ending their break with laughs, and they looked forward to settling the pizza debate. As they walked to the next class, the funny arguments continued, making the time between classes full of laughter and turning these ordinary moments into lasting memories of their college days.

In the lively lunch break at the cafeteria, Alex couldn't help but notice a girl across the courtyard. Her laughter and easygoing vibe caught his attention, creating a momentary pause in the routine of his day. Though he quickly refocused on grabbing lunch, there was something about her that left a sweet imprint on his thoughts. As he stood in line, the memory of that brief encounter lingered, a gentle spark that hinted at the possibility of something more in the days ahead, adding a subtle touch of anticipation to his college experience.

As the final lecture wrapped up, Alex and Marc found themselves in the quieting courtyard, backpacks in tow. The college day had run its course, leaving behind the rustle of leaves and the distant hum of the city. With tired yet content expressions, they exchanged nods, acknowledging the day's routine and the shared moments of laughter and then went their separate ways.

As Alex lay down on his bed at night, the day's memories swirled in his mind, and among them, the image of the girl from lunch held a quiet allure. In the stillness of his room, with the city's hum as his companion, he pondered the gentle mystery she brought to his day. The night wrapped around him like a blanket, and as he closed his eyes, a glimpse into the tapestry of Alex's world appeared — a blend of college adventures, family bonds, and the subtle interplay of daily happenings—

"Urban Symphony..!"

CHAPTER TWO

Her

In college, on another day that began just like any other, Alex moved through his usual routine—attending lectures, chatting in the cafeteria with Marc , and navigating the bustling hallways filled with the chatter of students. But life, as it often does, had a way of surprising him. During the break between classes, as he rounded a corner near the library, he found himself face-to-face with the girl from the canteen. She was walking from the opposite direction, carrying a stack of books and wearing a bright smile that seemed to carry the warmth of the autumn sun. Their eyes met briefly, and for a moment, it felt as if time slowed. "Sorry!" they both said simultaneously, stepping aside awkwardly to let the other pass. Their shared laughter broke the ice, and her cheerful voice lingered in his mind long after she walked away into the library. He stood there for a second, caught off guard by the encounter, wondering what it was about her that seemed so familiar yet so intriguing.

Later that day, during a particularly dull math lecture, the classroom door swung open, grabbing everyone's attention. Heads turned, glad for a distraction, as the same girl entered, holding a stack of colorful flyers. "Sorry to interrupt, sir! I just need a minute to talk about the upcoming college festival," she announced with a smile that seemed to light up the entire room. As she handed out flyers, her enthusiasm was infectious, her energy waking up even the sleepiest students. When she reached Alex's row, their fingers brushed briefly as she passed him a flyer. "Hope to see you there," she said with a grin before moving on, leaving him with a racing heart and a smile he couldn't quite shake. Marc, sitting beside him, noticed the dreamy look on his face and smirked knowingly, nudging him. "Love's kicking down the door, isn't it?" Alex rolled his eyes, but deep down, he knew there was no denying it.

That evening, as Alex sat under an old oak tree in the courtyard with a book in hand, he noticed her again. She was sitting a few benches away, flipping through a novel, completely engrossed. Gathering his courage, he walked over and cleared his throat. "Hey," he said, holding up his book, "looks like we share the same habit of getting lost in stories." She looked up, surprised at first, but then smiled warmly. "Seems like it," she replied, tilting her head to read the title of his book. "Good choice." What began as a casual comment turned into a lively conversation. They bonded over their favorite stories, the ones they loved and the ones they didn't, and their laughter blended with the rustling leaves, creating a moment that felt like it belonged to that golden autumn day. "By the way, I'm Alex," he said with a playful grin. "And I've been meaning to ask—what's the name behind that captivating smile of yours?" She laughed, a little shy but amused, and replied, **Lisa.** And for the record, your pickup lines could use some work." That small exchange, full of teasing and lightheartedness, marked the beginning of a special connection.

Over the next two months, Alex and Lisa became inseparable. They spent hours talking under the oak tree, sharing jokes and dreams, and finding comfort in each other's company. When the college festival approached, the two exchanged a glance and instantly decided to be part of it together. The idea of performing a couple's dance felt thrilling, and neither could resist the chance to share the stage. On the night of the festival, the campus came alive with fairy lights, music, and excitement. As Alex and Lisa stepped onto the stage, the opening chords of "Night Changes" by One Direction began to play. They moved gracefully to the rhythm, their chemistry evident in every step, captivating the audience. In the middle of the performance, Alex twirled her into his arms, and as the music softened, he dropped to one knee.

"There's something I've been meaning to say," he began, looking into her eyes. "You've made my life brighter, funnier, and so much more interesting. Will you let me keep being the guy who makes you smile?" The crowd erupted in cheers, but for them, it felt like they were the only two people in the world. With a beaming smile and a nod, she gave her answer, and the moment was pure magic. Meanwhile, in the audience, Marc was busy capturing every second of the heartwarming scene on his iPhone, grinning ear to ear.

That night became more than just a memory—it became the start of their story, filled with laughter, love, and promises of more magical moments to come. The applause from the audience echoed the rhythm of their connection, leaving everyone who witnessed it with a smile and a belief in the beauty of serendipity.

CHAPTER THREE

Whispers of the Unknown

After dinner, Alex and Marc sat on the rooftop, enjoying the cool night breeze. The city lights sparkled in the distance, and a playful smile spread across Marc's face. With a chuckle, he said, "Hey, remember that last-day drama? You suddenly turned into this romantic hero, like some movie scene with background music, and bam! You proposed to your girl..! I swear, even the stars blinked in surprise!"

Alex laughed, his cheeks turning red. He tried to brush it off, but the memory made him smile. Deep down, though, his thoughts drifted elsewhere. Noticing this, Marc leaned in and asked, "What's on your mind? You're smiling, but it seems like there's something else you're thinking about."After a pause, Alex glanced toward the mountain behind their college. "Do you ever wonder what's on that mountain? The one at the back?" he asked.

Marc's eyes widened. "Wait, are you talking about the spooky backside of the mountain? The one with all those creepy stories? You can't be serious!""I think we should check it out," Alex replied with excitement.Marc shook his head. "That place is bad news! Nobody goes there, and for good reason!"Despite his protests, Alex convinced him after some back-and-forth, promising it would be a fun adventure. Reluctantly, Marc agreed, though he clearly wasn't thrilled about the idea. They decided to set out the next morning.

The next day, the two met at Marc's house, which was closer to the mountain. As they started climbing, the mountain seemed much more beautiful than they had imagined. The trees were tall, the flowers colorful, and the sound of birds filled the air. It felt peaceful, nothing like the spooky stories people told.Alex led the way, his excitement growing with every step. He smiled as he said, "See? Not so scary, right?"Marc tried to relax, but he kept glancing around nervously. "Yeah, but it's not the front side of the mountain that people talk about. It's the back that's supposed to be cursed.As they walked deeper into the forest, the path became narrow and uneven. The air grew cooler, and the silence was broken only by the occasional rustling of leaves. Alex slowed down, his eyes scanning the trees ahead.

"You feel that?" he asked, glancing back at Marc. Feel what?" Marc asked, looking uneasy.I don't know. It's like... the air's different here. Heavier, maybe," Alex replied, his tone thoughtful.Marc sighed.Great, Heavy air and creepy vibes. Just what we needed.

They kept moving, their footsteps crunching softly on the dry leaves. Alex was quiet, his gaze fixed ahead, as if something was pulling him forward. After a few moments, he stopped and turned to his friend.

"Hey, what if all those stories were true? What if there's actually something here—something people were never meant to find?" he asked, his voice low.Marc rolled his eyes but couldn't hide his curiosity. "Well, let's hope whatever it is doesn't bite. Come on, let's keep moving before I change my mind.The two shared a nervous laugh and continued walking. The trees seemed to close in around them, and the faint smell of damp earth filled the air. As they rounded a bend, something caught their attention—a faint glow coming from somewhere further up the trail.

You see that? Alex asked, his voice barely above a whisper.Marc nodded, his expression tense. "Yeah. I see it.

They exchanged a look, a mix of fear and excitement, before cautiously moving toward the light. Whatever was waiting for them, they knew there was no turning back now.Their simple adventure had just turned into something far bigger than they could have imagined.

CHAPTER FOUR

The Puzzling Peaks

As Alex and Marc continued their trek up the mountain's backside, an eerie sense of mystery settled over them. The path grew narrower, and the lively sounds of nature slowly faded into an unsettling silence. The air felt charged, almost alive, as though something unseen was watching their every move. Each step seemed to carry them deeper into a world untouched by time. The occasional rustle of leaves and faint, unidentifiable sounds only heightened the strange atmosphere, transforming their casual adventure into something much more intriguing. They had no idea that the mountain's heart was holding secrets, ancient and unexplored, waiting for them to stumble upon.

Stopping to catch their breath, Marc couldn't contain his curiosity any longer. "Hey, buddy, what's the deal? How did we go from rooftop talks to hiking the creepy side of this mountain? I mean, seriously, what made you pick the mysterious backside? I thought we were all about enjoying scenic views!" He grinned, genuinely intrigued. Alex chuckled, looking ahead at the winding path. "I don't know. It's like this itch, you know? That feeling there's something more, something hidden. And all those spooky tales about this side of the mountain? They just made it impossible to resist. I thought, why not? Let's make some stories of our own." Their conversation was lighthearted, filled with laughter, but their surroundings carried a weight of anticipation, as if something extraordinary was just ahead.

While walking, Marc suddenly froze and pointed toward a massive rock nearby. "Hey, look at that! Behind the rock—something's shining!" he whispered, his voice laced with a mix of excitement and fear. Sure enough, a faint, flickering light glimmered in the distance, just out of reach. Both of them felt their curiosity spike, and they cautiously moved closer to investigate. However, as Alex tiptoed toward the light, an unsettling sensation crept over him. It felt as though someone—or something—was watching them from the dark jungle. He turned around quickly, scanning the trees, but found nothing except the unnerving stillness of the forest. The silence around them deepened, amplifying the sound of their own breathing.

As they reached the source of the flickering glow, Marc noticed something half-buried in the dirt near the rock. It was a broken piece of an ancient symbol, its edges worn and glowing faintly. The design was intricate, as though it belonged to an era long forgotten. Both of them exchanged wide-eyed glances, realizing they had uncovered something far beyond their imagination. The forest seemed to hold its breath, the air thick with an unexplainable energy. Just as Marc leaned down to pick it up, a sudden jolt of electric energy shot through him. The shock was so powerful that it sent him flying backward, landing with a loud thud several feet away. The glowing symbol dimmed instantly, as though it had expelled all its energy.

Alex sprinted to Marc, heart pounding in his chest. Marc was lying on the ground, stunned and visibly shaken, but thankfully, still conscious. "Are you okay? Say something!" Alex asked, his voice filled with panic. Slowly, Marc opened his eyes, groaning as he tried to sit up. Though he had a few minor injuries, he managed a weak smile to reassure his friend. The supernatural power they had just encountered, coupled with the oppressive silence of the forest, sent chills down their spines. Realizing the danger they were in, the pair decided to abandon their exploration. Together, they hurried down the mountain, leaving behind the mysterious artifact and the unsettling aura of the mountain's backside. However, as they made their way home, a single thought lingered in their minds—what had they stumbled upon, and why did it feel like the mountain wasn't done with them yet...

CHAPTER FIVE

Echoes of Curiosity and Comfort

Unable to hold it in any longer, Alex decided to share his thoughts with Lisa. That evening, they met at their favorite spot in the park, a cozy bench under a canopy of leafy trees. The soft golden light of the setting sun painted her face as she smiled at him, sensing something unusual in his demeanor.

"Okay, spill it," she said with a teasing grin. "You've been weirdly quiet today. What's going on in that mysterious brain of yours?"

At first, he hesitated, the weight of the story making it difficult to start. But as the words tumbled out, her playful demeanor shifted. He described everything—the mountain trek, the eerie flickering light, the ancient symbol, and the force that had left his best friend injured. He even admitted his growing obsession with the artifact and the feeling that it was meant for him to find.

For a moment, she burst out laughing.

"You're kidding, right? This sounds like something out of those superhero comics you love," she said, shaking her head.

But the intensity in his eyes stopped her mid-laugh. Her amusement gave way to concern as she realized he wasn't joking.

"Wait, you're serious?"

"Dead serious," he replied. "I can't explain it, but it's like... it's pulling me back. I know it sounds crazy, but I feel like I'm supposed to go back."

His voice carried a mix of conviction and unease, making her realize this wasn't just an adventure gone wrong—it was something deeper.

Her expression softened, and she gently placed her hand over his, intertwining their fingers in a comforting gesture.

"I believe you," she said, her voice low and sincere, her eyes searching his for any trace of doubt.

"But it scares me, too. What if it's dangerous? What if something happens to you? You said your best friend got hurt. I don't want that to happen to you. I can't lose you."

She squeezed his hand, her touch grounding him amidst the storm of thoughts swirling in his mind.

"I'll come with you," she added softly after a pause, her determination evident despite the fear in her voice. "You shouldn't face this alone. If something happens, I want to be there for you."

Her offer made his heart ache with a mix of gratitude and worry. He looked at her, her unwavering support warming him in ways he couldn't describe. But the memory of Marc being thrown back by the symbol flashed through his mind. The thought of Lisa being in harm's way was unbearable.

"No," he said firmly, though his voice carried the weight of his concern. "I can't let you come with me. It's too dangerous. I saw what happened to Marc—whatever this is, it's not normal. I need to figure this out, but I can't risk you getting hurt. I'd never forgive myself if something happened to you."

Her expression faltered for a moment, but she nodded, understanding his reasoning even if it scared her to let him go alone.

"Fine," she whispered, her voice trembling slightly. "But promise me something. No matter what, you'll come back to me. I don't care what you find or what happens—just come back. I'll always be here for you, no matter what."

He gave her hand a gentle squeeze, feeling a rush of comfort from her words.

"I promise," he said, his voice steady despite the turmoil inside. For the first time that day, he felt a flicker of peace, knowing that no matter where this journey led, he wouldn't truly be alone.

The next morning, despite her words of encouragement, Alex found it difficult to focus on the mundane rhythm of his day. His mind kept wandering back to the mountain, to the flickering light behind the rock, and to the broken symbol that seemed to hold answers to questions he couldn't yet articulate. He tried to act normal, even sharing a few laughs with Lisa, but his resolve to return to the mountain alone was growing stronger with every passing moment.

Though she didn't say it out loud, he could see in her eyes that she was still worried about him. Her quiet support gave him strength, even as he made up his mind to keep her away from whatever danger awaited him. As the day wore on, he quietly prepared himself for the journey back, knowing that this time, he would face the unknown alone.

CHAPTER SIX

The Chosen Path

The decision to return to the mountain had been a silent one. Alex needed answers, and he needed them alone. The trek back was nerve-wracking, each step weighed down by the memories of his injured friend and the inexplicable pull of the artifact. The sun dipped below the horizon as he arrived at the site, painting the sky in ominous shades of orange and purple. The flickering light behind the stone was still there, pulsing like a heartbeat. His own heartbeat mirrored it, erratic and fast.

He stood frozen for a moment, nerves paralyzing him. The memory of Marc being thrown back replayed in his mind like a warning. But the pull of curiosity and destiny was stronger. Gritting his teeth, he forced himself forward and reached out. His fingers brushed against the mysterious structure, and the light stopped blinking. He braced himself for the worst, but nothing happened. No force threw him back, no pain coursed through him. Instead, an silence enveloped the area.

Cautiously, he examined the artifact. It was a strange, jagged piece of what seemed like crystal, radiating a soft glow. He carefully placed it in his bag, his instincts screaming at him to leave immediately. Yet, as he turned to leave, the feeling of being watched returned. His breath hitched as he scanned the area, every shadow suddenly seeming alive. Then he spotted him—a frail, old man standing under a tree, his figure barely discernible in the fading light.

Fear gripped him, but the man spoke before he could react. ***"Finally, the chosen one is here to save us."***

His voice was raspy but carried an undeniable authority. The old man gestured for him to follow, and though every logical fiber in his body screamed at him to run, something about the man's presence was compelling. Against his better judgment, he followed.The journey was arduous. The old man led him through dense jungle paths and across streams that seemed to appear out of nowhere. The forest grew darker and more foreboding with each step, the air thick with tension. Yet the old man pressed on, his frail body moving with surprising agility. Finally, they arrived at a small, ancient house nestled deep within the wilderness. It was unassuming, almost forgotten, with just a water tank, a smoldering fire, a rudimentary sleeping area, and a few boxes.

"Please, sit. We have much to discuss," the old man said, gesturing toward a simple wooden stool.Alex hesitated but eventually sat down, his eyes darting around the room. The atmosphere was heavy, almost oppressive, as though the walls themselves carried secrets.This place... it's quite different from what I expected," he said, trying to mask his unease. "Why did you bring me here? And who are you? You mentioned I'm the 'chosen one.' What does that mean? Why am I here?" His questions spilled out, a mix of confusion and frustration.The old man leaned forward, his expression unreadable. "In time, you will come to understand the weight of that title. For now, know this: the fate of our world rests in your hands. I am **Nyro,** This house has been my sanctuary and a place of preparation for this moment.The absurdity of the situation overwhelmed him, and he let out a nervous laugh. "Okay, so you're telling me I'm some kind of superhero destined to save the world? This is a joke, right?"

"It may sound incredible, but it is the truth," Nyro replied, his voice unwavering. "Your role is crucial. You have strengths and abilities that you are yet to discover. I will guide you in harnessing these powers and preparing for the battles ahead.""Battles? What kind of challenges am I going to face?" he asked, his skepticism fading as the Nyro's serious demeanor began to sink in. Nyro's face grew solemn as he spoke, his words heavy with forewarning. "You must understand the gravity of the situation. The villain who once terrorized this world is not merely a distant memory. Before they left Earth, they made a chilling vow: 'I will return in 500 years. Until then, I will travel across the cosmos, destroying every planet I encounter. I will spend this time in penance and training, becoming the greatest force in the universe. By the time I come back, no one will have the courage to stand against me. My dream is to annihilate this world and all others.'The weight of the revelation left Alex reeling. The idea of facing someone who had spent centuries growing stronger, someone whose sole purpose was destruction, was incomprehensible.They are not just a conqueror," Nyro continued.They are a destroyer. Their goal is to impose their will on every world, to obliterate any resistance. When they return, they will be an unstoppable force unless someone rises to meet them.Why me? Alex asked, his voice barely above a whisper. "Why am I the one who has to stop them?"Because you are the only one who can," Nyro replied. "You have a power within you that must be developed. It will be a long and arduous journey, but with determination and proper guidance, you can become the hero needed to face this impending doom."The seriousness of Nyro's words finally broke through his disbelief. The enormity of what lay ahead began to settle in, leaving him both terrified and resolute. The path before him was unclear, but one thing was certain—his life would never be the same.

The Map to Destiny

The next evening, Alex decided he couldn't bear the weight of the mysterious events alone. He called Lisa and Marc, asking them to meet at their usual spot in the park—a secluded corner with a view of the lake, a place brimming with memories both comforting and challenging.As he approached, Lisa sat on the weathered bench, concern etched across her face, while his best friend Marc stood nearby, arms crossed, radiating skepticism."You're late," Marc snapped as Alex settled into the empty space beside Lisa. "And you've got a lot of explaining to do.""I know, I know," he said, raising his hands in surrender. "Just... hear me out."He began recounting the events of the previous night—the strange blinking artifact he found, the enigmatic old man who revealed fragments of a chilling prophecy, and the trek through the jungle that had led him to the artifact. As he spoke, he pulled the mysterious piece from his bag and placed it in front of them. Its faint glow bathed the bench in an otherworldly light."This is what I found," he said softly.His girlfriend gasped, staring at the artifact with wide eyes, while Marc's suspicion turned into fear as he alreaddy experianced the effect of that symbol.When the story ended, a heavy silence hung in the air.

"You're telling me you went back there alone?" Marc finally exploded. "After everything? And you found... that?" He gestured at the glowing piece. "What if something had happened to you as well? You should've called me!""I didn't want to drag you into something dangerous again," Alex replied, guilt evident in his tone."That's not your call to make!" Marc snapped. "We've been through everything together. You don't get to shut me out like that."

Lisa intervened, gently placing a hand on the Marc's arm. "I get why you're upset, but let's focus on what matters. If this is real—and I think it is—we're dealing with something much bigger than us." She turned to Alex. "What did the old man say to do next? His name is Nyro,He said I need to train. To figure out my powers and prepare for whatever's coming," Alex admitted.

Marc sighed, rubbing his temples. This is insane. Powers? Training? A world-ending villain? We're not superheroes.Maybe we don't have all the answers," Lisa said, "but we can't ignore this either. If this villain is coming back, we need to figure out what we can do. Together. The trio exchanged determined glances.Then we start by talking to the old man," Alex said. "He knows more than he's told me.

The Old Man's Tale

The next morning, they arrived at the Nyro's secluded home deep in the forest. His modest dwelling, filled with ancient artifacts and scrolls, seemed like a fragment of another world. The old man greeted them with a knowing look, his expression heavy with the burden of truths long concealed.

Alex wasted no time. "I've told them everything. They need to know more—about you, the symbol, and what we're really up against."

Nyro sighed, motioning for them to sit. Picking up a tattered scroll from a nearby table, he began unraveling a tale long buried by time.

"Long ago," he began, his voice laden with the weight of centuries, "my people discovered the Symbol of Aegis. It wasn't just a relic; it was a celestial artifact that connected us to the energy of the cosmos. This symbol wasn't forged by mortal hands but was a gift left by an advanced race to protect Earth from universal threats. It contained three distinct energies: **light, strength, and wisdom**. Together, these energies could repel even the most powerful foes."When the villains arrived, they sought to destroy the symbol, knowing it was our only defense. I led my people into battle, wielding the symbol's power myself. But its energy was too great for any one person. I could not control it fully, and in my failure, the villains shattered it into three pieces. They scattered the fragments across the world to ensure no one could unite its power again. As punishment for resisting them, they cursed me with eternal life—a life meant to witness Earth's decay and despair while they ravaged other planets."

"Wait... ancient?" Marc interrupted, his brow furrowed. "What are you saying? How old are you?" Nyro smiled faintly, though it carried no joy. "My age? Infinity. I have been alive long enough to see countless empires rise and fall. My punishment and curse is to watch the world crumble, awaiting the day these villains return. *"I was the king of the ancient place on the earth but when villains came on earth to distroy and ruins the planet, i lost the battle and villains gives curse to me that you will never ever die and will take taste of the defeat of this world until i came here again from destroying other planets too."*

The revelation left the group stunned, but Nyro continued."The first piece," he said, gesturing to a fragment resting on a pedestal, "was entrusted to me by the remnants of my people. It's been my burden to guard it through the ages. The second piece found its way to the ruins of my kingdom, hidden in the debris of our last stand. That is the piece you hold now," he said, nodding at the artifact in the Alex's hands."The final piece," he said gravely, "was carried to an island far beyond the reach of ordinary men. One of my most trusted knights fled there during the battle, knowing the villains would not stop hunting it. He entrusted the island's guardians to hide it so well that only the truly worthy could retrieve it. Generations have passed, and the guardians have grown more cautious. To retrieve it, you'll need this map.He handed them a worn parchment, its edges frayed from time. The map depicted a treacherous journey across seas and through uncharted territories, with cryptic symbols marking the island's location."The path ahead is perilous," Nyro warned. "But if you fail to retrieve the final piece and unite the symbol, the villains will have no opposition when they return.

CHAPTER EIGHT

Festive Night

The town was alive with excitement as Carnival arrived. Bright lights, colorful decorations, and the sounds of laughter and music filled the streets. It was the one time of the year when everyone in the city came together to celebrate, forgetting all their worries. The smell of delicious street food, the sparkle of firecrackers, and the cheerful dances made it a festival to remember.

The day began with the Alex waking up early. He stretched, feeling a mix of excitement and nerves from the strange dream the night before. Shaking off the thought, he went to the kitchen to wish his mother and sister a happy Carnival. Happy Carnival, Mom, Sis! he said with a warm smile. His sister playfully threw a cushion at him. Happy Carnival to you too!" they both replied with joy. During breakfast, he called Lisa. "What are you wearing today?" he asked, trying to sound casual.

Why? Planning to match?she teased. "Of course!" Let's be the best-looking couple in town, he replied, grinning.Okay, fine,she laughed. "I'll wear something white."

By 5 o'clock, the plan was set. Alex, Marc, and Lisa were meeting in front of Marc's house. As he waited, he saw her walking toward them. She was wearing the prettiest white dress he had ever seen, and it looked as if it was made just for her.She smiled shyly. "How do I look?" she asked, tilting her head slightly.

He was completely mesmerized. "Beautiful," he said softly, unable to look away.

She blushed a little and smiled. "You're looking handsome as always," she said, her voice soft but sincere.Marc rolled his eyes and grinned. "Alright, we get it—you two are the picture-perfect couple. But can we stop this love fest and actually enjoy the festival?"All three of them looked fantastic, dressed in their best outfits for Carnival. Together, they set out to make it a night to remember.The streets were packed with people. They started to greet friends, neighbors, and even strangers.Firecrackers lit up the atmosphere with bursts of vivid colors, their echoes blending with the rhythmic beats of drums and cheerful music. There was music everywhere, and everyone was dancing.

As they strolled, a street performer began playing a familiar tune—*Perfect by Ed Sheeran*. Alex and Lisa exchanged a glance and smiled."Shall we?" she asked playfully.

He took her hand, and they began to dance in the middle of the street. Their movements were natural and in sync, just like in the college function where they had danced together for the first time. The memory flashed through his mind, filling him with warmth.The crowd around them clapped and cheered, creating a magical moment. To him, it felt like time had stopped, and it was just the two of them, moving to the rhythm of the song.Their dance ended with a shared laugh, and they rejoined their friends, who teased them endlessly.From there, the group joined in with the crowd, dancing with the people, eating delicious food, and setting off firecrackers. It felt like the perfect night.

But then, something strange happened.

While they were walking down a brightly lit street, Alex suddenly froze. Across the crowd, he saw a familiar face—the same man from his dream. The man was standing there, watching him.Without thinking, he started running toward the man. "Wait! Stop!" he shouted, pushing through the crowd.The man turned and started walking away quickly. Alex tried to follow, but the streets were too crowded, and he lost sight of him. Breathing heavily, he stood in the middle of the street, confused and worried.

When he returned to Marc, He asked, Where did you disappear to? We thought you got lost!

"I saw him," he said, his voice filled with tension. "The man from my dream. He was here!"

Marc laughed nervously. "You're probably just imagining things. Maybe it's the festival vibe. Chill out!"But Alex was sure of what he saw.As the night went on, they tried to enjoy the festival again, but Alex couldn't shake off the uneasy feeling.The streets were still buzzing with energy from the festival, but in this quiet corner, everything felt different. It was late at night, and most of the crowds had gone home. Only the soft glow of the streetlamp lit up the space around them, casting long shadows on the empty road. Alex and Lisa were alone as Marc went to home with his mother for help.

Alex took a deep breath and began to explain what had happened. He told her about the man he had seen on the streets—the same man from his dream who had warned him.I know this sounds weird," he said, his voice shaky. "But I swear, it was him. I saw him in the crowd. He just disappeared when I tried to follow him.

She listened carefully, her face calm and understanding. She put a hand on his arm, offering comfort. "It might just be your mind playing tricks on you," she said gently. "Or maybe it's something else. Either way, don't worry. We'll figure it out. I'm here with you."

Hearing her words made him feel a little better. The tension in his chest eased. He looked at her, grateful for the way she always knew how to comfort him. It was one of the reasons he loved her so much—she was always there for him, no matter what.

"Thanks," he whispered, smiling softly. "I feel better now."

She smiled back, her eyes full of warmth and care. Without saying another word, she took a small step closer to him. He could feel her breath on his skin, warm and sweet. For a moment, everything else disappeared. The quiet night, the empty streets—they were the only ones who mattered in that moment.Slowly, he leaned in, closing the distance between them. Their lips met in a soft, gentle kiss. It was slow, tender, like a promise they didn't need to say aloud. After a moment, they pulled back slightly, looking into each other's eyes. Without saying anything, they both knew how they felt.He pulled her closer, deepening the kiss. It felt right, like nothing else mattered in the world except for the two of them standing there, alone under the streetlamp..!

CHAPTER NINE

Another Side & The Unspoken Promise

The morning sun streamed through the curtains of Alex's small room, casting a warm glow over the scattered papers and books on his desk. He stretched lazily, the weight of the past few days making his muscles ache. The sound of his mother bustling in the kitchen and his sister humming a tune brought a fleeting sense of normalcy to his mind.

He joined his family for breakfast—a simple yet comforting meal of freshly baked bread and warm tea. His mother asked him about the carnival, and he recounted the lighter moments with a small smile, sparing them the details of the strange man. His sister, as usual, teased him about his girlfriend, making him chuckle despite himself.

Later in the day, he found himself back in his room, staring at the pieces of the symbol and the map on his desk. The unease he felt the night before returned, stronger than ever. Something about the strange man's appearance gnawed at him, and he knew he wouldn't find peace until he sought answers.

By nightfall, he was climbing the familiar path to the Nyro's mountain refuge. The journey felt heavier this time, his mind filled with questions and doubts. When he arrived, Nyro was already waiting, seated near the crackling fire with an air of quiet anticipation.

"I felt you would return," Nyro said, motioning for the Alex to sit."I need to understand," Alex began, his voice trembling slightly. "There's a man... I saw him during the festival. He was in my dream, warning me. And then I saw him in the crowd too. Who is he?"

Nyro's expression darkened, and he took a deep breath. "You saw a messenger of the shadows," he said, his voice grave. "He is **Renox's** agent— **Raegar,**a man who exists to carry out his will and spread his reach. If he has appeared before you, it means Renox knows of your quest."

"Renox?, Raegar?" Alex repeated,a chill running down his spine.

Nyro leaned forward, his face illuminated by the firelight. "Raegar is the ruler of the Castle of Hell, a place shrouded in eternal darkness. His power comes from the shadows themselves—the darker the place, the stronger he becomes. Long ago, he was human, but he was consumed by his ambition to control all light and life. Through the Shadow Relic, he gained his powers, but it twisted him into something monstrous."

Why does he want the symbol?" Alex asked, his hands tightening into fists.

The symbol you seek is the one thing that can challenge his dominion," Nyro explained. "When completed, it can summon the Light Core, a source of pure light powerful enough to destroy him and his empire. That is why he will stop at nothing to ensure you fail.

Alex's breath hitched. "And the strange man... he's helping Renox? He was in my dream, warning me I'd lose someone close to me."

Nyro nodded solemnly. "Raegar,He serves Renox, but his words are not without meaning. Renox thrives on fear and despair. He will try to break you, to make you lose hope. You must stay strong, for the path ahead will not be easy."

The fire crackled between them as the Nyro's words sank deep into the Alex's mind. The road ahead was clear now, but it was also darker than ever before.As he left the mountains and made his way back to the town, Alex couldn't shake the feeling that the shadows were watching him, waiting for their chance to strike.

Meanwhile — another side where light dares to reach...

Far from the fading sun and the warm earth, deep beneath the Castle of Hell, a storm brewed in silence.

Reagar stood alone inside a colossal chamber — walls etched with runes, air thick with shadows. At the center burned a pit of black flame, and within it, a faint echo pulsed — a voice not heard, but felt. It was **Renox**.

"He resists the fear," Reagar muttered, his jaw tight. "Even after the warning."

The flame pulsed. A shape flickered within — Renox, distorted and immense, cloaked in ash and fury.

"Of course he does," the voice hissed, ancient and bitter. "That's what makes him dangerous."

"He is close to the final piece," Reagar said. "The map is nearly complete. The girl and the friend are still with him. I sense the old man's protection."

Renox stepped from the flame — not in body, but in essence — a swirl of armor and shadows that darkened the very air.
"Hope still shields him. That must change."

Reagar's eyes flicked to the symbol carved into the obsidian altar.
"He dreams of victory. He believes light will save him."

"Then we show him what light costs."

A silence passed — then Renox raised a hand and whispered something ancient.

A ripple surged across the room.
A shadow on the wall shifted. Twitched.

And opened its eyes.

"Send it," Renox commanded. "No more warnings. No more dreams."

His voice cracked like thunder.
"Let him bleed before the battle even begins."

Back in the world above, the winds shifted. And somewhere far away, Alex felt the faintest chill brush his spine — as if something had begun moving in the dark.

The Unspoken Promise...

Under the golden rays of the setting sun, the trio sat on their favorite spot—a quiet hill overlooking the bustling city below. It had always been their place for heart-to-heart talks, and tonight, the air was heavy with a sense of foreboding. The Carnival festivities had come and gone, leaving behind an eerie calm that seemed to echo the thoughts running through their minds.

Breaking the silence, Alex cleared his throat. "I need to tell you both something." He paused, glancing at Marc and Lisa. "The time has come... I have to go after the final piece. Without it, everything we've been through will mean nothing."

His words hung in the air like a storm cloud. Marc leaned forward, frowning. "You're not seriously thinking of going alone, are you? That's insane. You have no idea what's waiting for you out there."

"I do know," Alex replied firmly, gripping the edges of the map. "That's why I have to go alone. This is my fight, my destiny."

"You're forgetting something," Marc argued, his voice rising slightly. "We've been with you through everything. You don't have to face this alone. I'll come with you—no arguments."

Alex froze for a moment, his friend's words sparking an unwanted memory. He closed his eyes, recalling the chilling warning from the strange man in his dream: "You'll lose your loved ones."

He whispered almost inaudibly, "Don't..." Then he looked up, his gaze piercing but filled with a quiet plea. "Don't come with me. Please."

Marc's expression hardened. "Why? Why are you pushing us away now? You wouldn't understand, Alex said, his voice trembling slightly but resolute. "If something happens to you because of me... I can't live with that.

Silence fell, heavy and unbreakable. Lisa reached out to touch his hand, but he pulled away, unable to meet her eyes. Standing abruptly, he muttered, "I'll go alone. This is final."

Without another word, he walked off, leaving the two of them behind. Marc clenched his fists, frustration bubbling inside him. Lisa sighed, her heart aching as she watched him disappear into the distance.

The next morning, Alex packed his belongings carefully. With both pieces of the symbol safely tucked away and the ancient map clutched tightly in his hand, he left his home, determination etched on his face.

But, his best friend had no intention of letting him go alone. Hiding in the shadows, Marc silently traced the Alex's path, keeping a careful distance.

The journey began under a sky that shifted from pale blue to steel gray, as if nature itself sensed the storm brewing. Alex's focus was unwavering, but little did he know, danger lurked closer than he anticipated. And in the distance, his best friend followed, torn between loyalty and fear.

For now, the path to the last piece of symbol lay ahead, riddled with mysteries and challenges. But behind him, the unseen bond of friendship whispered a silent promise: You will not face this alone.

CHAPTER TEN

Shivpura : The First Step

The sun was just beginning to rise, casting an orange hue across the sky, as the old, rickety bus pulled into the station. Its paint was peeling, and the windows rattled every time the engine groaned. The destination was painted in faded letters on the front," Shivpura", a small, forgotten village nestled at the base of the mountains. This was where the journey truly began.

Alex stepped onto the bus, clutching the fragile map tightly in his hand. His heart raced with a mix of excitement and fear. Nyro's words echoed in his mind: "This map will lead you to what you seek, but the path is not easy. Trust yourself." He scanned the seats, most of which were torn or patched with mismatched fabric. Finding an empty spot near the window, he settled in, his bag resting on his lap.

As the bus roared to life, a plume of black smoke erupted from its exhaust. It jolted forward, making everyone inside sway. Alex stared out of the window, watching his town fade into the distance. This might be the last time he saw it, he thought. Doubts began creeping into his mind.

"Am I doing the right thing?" he wondered. "What if I fail? What if this map leads to nothing?" The weight of the journey ahead felt heavy on his shoulders. He thought about his family, his responsibilities, and the strange man's cryptic warning about losing someone close. The thought sent a chill down his spine.

The bus rattled along the uneven road, bouncing over potholes. The passengers were a mix of locals and travelers. Some carried bundles of goods, while others simply looked lost in their own worlds. Unbeknownst to the Alex, a familiar face sat quietly in the back of the bus. His best friend,Marc. concealed by a hooded jacket, watched him intently. Concern and determination flickered in his friend's eyes. He had followed him, unable to let him face this journey alone, even if it meant staying hidden.

Alex's thoughts drifted to the map. He unfolded it carefully, tracing the faint lines with his finger. The coded notes seemed to taunt him. The old man had given him hints, but deciphering them would require focus and patience. Each landmark on the map felt like a challenge waiting to be overcome. The river, the mountain, and finally, the distant island—it all seemed so far away. Yet, something deep inside him refused to give up.

I've come this far," he thought, clenching his fists. "I can't turn back now. If I don't try, I'll regret it forever.

Hours passed, and the landscape outside changed from bustling towns to vast, open fields. The bus stopped occasionally at small roadside stalls, where vendors sold steaming cups of tea and fried snacks. The protagonist stepped out during one such stop, stretching his legs. He noticed an old man selling handmade trinkets. One of them, a small wooden carving of a compass, caught his eye. He bought it, thinking it might bring him luck.

Back on the bus, the journey resumed. The road became narrower, winding through dense forests. The air grew cooler, and the sound of birds replaced the hum of city life. Alex felt a strange sense of calm despite the uncertainty ahead. He thought about his best friend and their countless adventures growing up.

"If only he were here," he sighed, unaware that his wish was closer to reality than he realized. In the back of the bus, Marc smiled faintly, hearing those words but staying hidden. He knew Alex would be furious if he discovered he had followed him. But he couldn't let him face this alone.

As Shivpura drew closer, the bus began to climb uphill. The engine groaned louder, struggling against the steep incline. The passengers braced themselves as the bus swayed precariously on the edge of the narrow road. Alex's heart pounded, but he forced himself to stay calm. He thought about the island and the final piece of the symbol. The image of the villain flashed in his mind, fueling his resolve.

"This is bigger than me," he realized. "If I don't do this, no one else will."

Finally, after what felt like an eternity, the bus screeched to a halt. The driver announced their arrival in Shivpura. Alex stepped off the bus, his legs stiff but his spirit unwavering. The village was quiet, with cobblestone streets and small houses surrounded by mist-covered hills. This was the starting point marked on the map.

In the shadows, Marc stepped off the bus too, careful to keep his distance. The journey had just begun, and both of them were ready to face whatever lay ahead—even if only one of them knew it.

Alex took a deep breath, clutching the map tightly. With one last look at the bus, he turned toward the path leading to the river. The challenges ahead were unknown, but his determination burned brighter than ever.Little did he know, the journey would test him in ways he could never imagine.

CHAPTER ELEVEN

The Journey Across the Sea

After leaving Shivpura behind, the road ahead was filled with uncertainty. The dusty paths turned into soft, wet sand as the sound of waves crashing against the shore grew louder. A vast, endless sea stretched in front of Alex, its deep blue waters reflecting the golden light of the setting sun. The journey had just begun, and already, the first challenge stood before him—a sea that needed to be crossed.

Standing at the shore, he saw a small dock where a few wooden boats were tied. The salty breeze carried the scent of the ocean, and the rhythmic sound of water hitting the boats created a strange sense of calm. But he didn't have time to admire the view. He needed to find a way to cross this sea and reach the mysterious island that the map pointed toward.

He walked toward the boats, scanning the area for someone who could help. Most of the fishermen and boatmen looked busy with their own work, preparing their boats or unloading their daily catch. After a few moments, his eyes landed on an old man sitting near a small wooden boat. The man had a long white beard, a tired face, and sharp, observant eyes that made him look like someone who had spent his entire life on these waters.

Alex approached him and asked, "Excuse me, can you take me across the sea?"

The old boatman looked up, his deep brown eyes narrowing slightly as he examined him from head to toe. He adjusted the cloth wrapped around his head and let out a small sigh before speaking. "Where exactly do you need to go, young man?"

He hesitated for a moment before pulling out the map from his bag. Unfolding it carefully, he pointed toward a small island marked in the middle of the sea. "I need to reach this island," he said, trying to keep his voice steady.

The boatman stared at the map for a long moment. His expression changed slightly, as if he recognized something but chose not to say it out loud. He finally leaned back against the wooden post and let out a dry chuckle. "You want to go there?" he said, shaking his head. "That's not a place for outsiders."

Hearing this, Alex's heart skipped a beat. He had expected challenges, but he didn't think the place itself would have such a reputation. "What do you mean?" he asked carefully.

The old man scratched his beard and sighed. "That island... it's not like other places. The people living there are different. They don't welcome strangers. If they see someone who doesn't belong, they will refuse to let them stay. Some even say they drive outsiders away by force."

A cold breeze brushed against the Alex's face as he processed the boatman's words. The situation was more complicated than he thought. But he had come too far to turn back now. He needed to find the last piece of the symbol, no matter what.

The boatman studied his face carefully and then asked, "Why do you need to go there?"

The question caught him off guard. His mind raced for an answer, but he knew he couldn't tell the truth. If he mentioned the symbol or the map, the boatman might refuse to take him or, worse, alert the people on the island.

Thinking quickly, he forced a small smile and said, "I'm a scientist. I'm researching the island's environment, studying its land and climate."

The boatman raised an eyebrow, clearly not convinced. "A scientist, huh?" he muttered. "Never heard of anyone researching that island before."

Alex shrugged, trying to appear calm. "Well, there's always a first time," he said with a small laugh.

The old man didn't laugh. Instead, he leaned forward slightly and lowered his voice. "Listen, boy," he said seriously. "That island is not just some normal piece of land. There's a reason why no one dares to go there. If you step foot on that island, you won't be welcomed. You might not even be allowed to leave."

His words sent a small shiver down the protagonist's spine, but he refused to show any fear. Instead, he simply looked the boatman in the eyes and said, "I will manage."

The boatman sighed again, rubbing his forehead as if he was debating whether to help or not. After a long silence, he finally said, "Alright... get in the boat."

With those words, **the journey across the sea** began. The sun dipped lower into the horizon, casting an orange glow over the waters. The boat rocked gently as the old man untied it from the dock and pushed it into the waves. With steady hands, he grabbed the oars and started rowing, guiding them toward the unknown.

The sea ahead was vast, and so was the uncertainty that came with it. But the Alex had no choice. He had to reach the island, no matter what awaited him there...

The boat moved slowly, cutting through the silent sea. The wooden oars splashed gently, breaking the stillness of the water. The island was still far, about 14-15 km ahead, but now it looked bigger, darker. The mountains stood tall in the background, their peaks lost in thick clouds.

The boatman kept rowing, his face calm but focused. Alex, sitting on an old oaken plank, felt a strange chill in the air. He pulled out the map again and traced his finger over it. Everything was happening exactly as shown—Shivpura, the sea, and now, the island ahead. But he knew this was just the beginning.

The silence between them stretched until the boatman finally spoke.

Boatman: "So... you still didn't tell me. Why do you really want to go there?"

Alex: "I told you already. I'm a scientist. I'm here for research."

Boatman (smirking): "A scientist, huh? Researching an island where no one is allowed?"

Alex didn't respond. He knew the boatman wasn't convinced, but he also knew that telling the truth would only make things worse.

As they moved closer, something unexpected happened.

A boat appeared in the distance, coming from the direction of the island. It was floating towards them. At first, it looked like just another empty boat, lost at sea. But as it came closer, Alex's eyes widened.

It wasn't just any boat.

It was their boat.

The same structure, the same oaken planks, even the same old rope tied to its side. It was exactly like the one they were sitting in.

But it was broken. Pieces of wood were cracked. Bloodstains covered the corners. And worst of all—it was completely empty.

It passed by them silently, as if it had already completed the journey they were about to take.

For a moment, Alex couldn't breathe. His mind raced with questions. Was this some kind of warning? Was this their future?

Alex turned to look at him, but just as he was about to speak—

The boat vanished.

One second, it was there. The next, it was gone.

The protagonist blinked. He looked around. The water was empty again. No broken boat. No blood. Just the open sea.

Alex (muttering to himself): "What... the hell...?"

He realized it was his illusion. A trick of the mind. A bhram. But why? Why did he see that? Was it his fear playing tricks on him, or was it something more?

The boatman looked at him, confused.

Boatman: "What happened?"

Alex (shaking his head): "Nothing... just my mind playing games."

But deep down, he knew—it wasn't just his mind. Something strange was happening. Something beyond logic.And they were heading straight towards it.

Two paths, one Destination..

The boat scraped against the sandy shore as they finally reached the island. The boatman pulled the oars in and tied the boat to a large rock. The protagonist climbed out and took his first steps onto the island's sand. A gentle breeze carried the salty scent of the sea, mixing with the fresh, earthy smell of the island's dense trees.

The boatman, still seated in the boat, looked at him with a stern, almost fatherly expression.

Boatman: "This is where my role ends, child. From here, you walk alone. Be careful—this place hides more than you can see."

Alex nodded, grateful for the help, and replied, "Thank you for bringing me here." The boatman simply nodded back, his eyes heavy with unspoken warnings.

As the boatman pushed away from the shore, Alex watched him row back toward the mainland. Alone now, he turned to face the island. At first glance, everything seemed normal. The soft sand beneath his feet, the thick trees ahead, and the calm, soothing air—all felt inviting, not threatening.

He unfolded the map again, checking his route. The map clearly showed the jungle ahead, and beyond it, the mountains and his final destination on the far side of the island.

Stepping forward, he entered the jungle. The canopy above was thick, blocking out much of the sunlight, making the air cooler. Leaves rustled softly, and distant bird calls echoed through the trees. It was peaceful, almost too peaceful.

Alex kept moving, following a narrow path worn into the ground. The deeper he went, the more he felt like the trees were watching him, their twisted branches reaching out like hands.

Meanwhile, the Best Friend's Journey..!

Unbeknownst to Alex, Marc was not far behind. The best friend had been careful, keeping a safe distance while ensuring he remained unseen. He had managed to find another boatman willing to take him across the sea, explaining that he was looking for his "reckless brother" who had gone ahead without him.

As the Marc crossed the sea, he couldn't help but feel uneasy. The ride was rougher than expected, with the waves growing larger the closer they got to the island. The boatman accompanying him was quieter, his eyes scanning the water nervously.

Halfway through their journey, Marc noticed something floating nearby. It was an old, empty boat, partially submerged with broken planks. A dark, red stain marked its edges.

Marc : "What happened to that boat?"

Boatman: "Bad things. Many come to this island, but not all return."

Marc (whispering to himself): "What have you gotten yourself into, man?"

The abandoned boat felt like a grim foreshadowing, but he pressed on, determined to reach his friend.

Reaching the Island

Once his boat reached the shore, Marc thanked the boatman and stepped onto the island. He scanned the sand, looking for footprints or any sign of his friend's path. The faint, fresh footprints in the sand led him into the jungle, and without hesitation, he followed.

Inside the jungle, every step felt heavier. The trees closed in, and the light dimmed. He could feel the weight of the island pressing down on him, but his resolve was unshaken.

Marc(muttering): "You're not facing this alone. Not while I'm here."

As Alex advanced through the dense foliage, his best friend trailed quietly behind, careful not to make a sound. Though separated by distance, both were heading toward the same unknown fate—a hidden world waiting to reveal its secrets.

The island may have seemed normal at first, but each step brought them closer to discovering the truth. The dense jungle, the eerie silence, and the ominous feeling in the air made it clear—this was not just another island.

Both of them, unaware of the other's presence, continued deeper into the heart of the island. Their paths ran parallel, destined to collide when they least expected it.

Destination..!

The jungle was deep and quiet, except for the soft sound of leaves rustling in the wind. The air felt heavy, filled with the scent of wet soil and old trees. Alex kept walking, his eyes on the path ahead, but his mind was somewhere else.

As he moved through the thick trees, his hand slipped into his pocket. His fingers touched something small and cold—**a bracelet.** Her bracelet. The one his girlfriend had given him before he left.

"You always chase strange things,"she had said, forcing a small smile. *"Just don't get lost in them."*

He exhaled slowly, gripping the bracelet for a moment before letting it go. **Was she thinking about him right now?** Did she regret not stopping him from leaving?

And what about his family? His mother, his father, his younger sister—they had no idea where he was. If something happened to him here, would they ever find out? Would they ever know what really happened?

A strange emptiness filled his chest, but he pushed it aside. **There was no turning back now.**

He took a deep breath and focused on the jungle ahead. The island still looked normal, but he knew that wouldn't last for long.

He took a deep breath and kept walking. The jungle still looked the same, but deep down, he knew it wouldn't stay that way for long.

Then something changed.

A faint sound came through the trees. It was low, like humming or whispering. He stopped and listened, trying to figure out where it was coming from. The jungle felt different now—like it was alive, like it was watching him.

He reached into his backpack and pulled out the folded paper—the one with the symbol. The same symbol that had led him here. It felt warm in his hands. The lines on it still didn't make full sense to him, but he knew it meant something important.

He looked behind him. The path he had come from was already fading into the trees. It was like the island was slowly closing in behind him.

A sound came from somewhere nearby. A stick breaking. Not loud, but clear.

He turned quickly. Nothing there.

He kept moving, slower now, until he stepped into a small clearing.

In the middle of it was an old stone structure. It looked like part of a building, maybe the top of a buried temple. Moss and vines covered most of it. Carved into the stone were symbols—one of them matched the one on his paper exactly.

He stared at it. His heart was beating faster now.

He took out the paper again. The symbol seemed to glow a little, even though the light around him was fading. The sky didn't change, but it felt like the world had gotten a bit darker. Like something had just noticed him.

He stood there, quiet. He could feel it in his bones—this was it.

He had reached the place he was meant to find.But what came next... he had no idea.

CHAPTER FOURTEEN

Fallen Guardian

The place was unlike anything Alex had seen before.

The structure rose out of the ground like it had been carved from a single, massive block of dark stone. There were no seams, no cracks — just one solid piece shaped into a strange, ancient form. Carvings covered the walls, glowing faintly with a dull blue light as he stepped closer. It felt like time stopped here. The air was still and thick.

He looked around, cautious, but everything was quiet. Then he saw it — the final piece of the symbol. It was set inside a stone altar at the center of the structure. Slowly, he walked toward it, each step echoing softly across the stone floor.

He didn't know he was being watched.

Not just by the eyes of the ancient people who lived in the shadows beyond the walls — but by two others. One hidden in loyalty. The other, in darkness.

Marc was not far — just behind a cluster of overgrown stone pillars. He had followed all the way here, staying out of sight. He wasn't sure why he came. Maybe he just couldn't let his friend do this alone. Maybe he just wanted to protect him one last time.

Then, he heard something.

A whisper in the air. A shift in the wind. And a movement.

The Reager,(Renox's agent)

That same man. The one Alex had seen in his dream. The one at the festival. He was here — moving quietly like a shadow, heading straight for the structure.

Marc's heart sank.

He looked back at the ancient building. His bestfriend Alex was just steps away from the final piece. But if the agent reached him in time, it would all be over. He knew what he had to do.

Without thinking, he ran.

He didn't charge straight into the Reager — he ran across the clearing loudly, making noise, snapping branches, breaking the silence. A moving distraction. Something to pull the Reager's focus.

And it worked.

Reager turned sharply, his head snapping toward the sound. His eyes locked onto the figure sprinting into the trees. A slow grin crawled across his face.

He followed.

The chase didn't last long.

Marc was fast, but the Reager was faster obviously.— and ruthless.

In the dense part of the jungle, just near the edge of a deep drop where the ground split into a dark pit, they clashed.

There were no words. Just movement. Punches. Dodges. A blur of fists and breath.

Marc held his own for a moment. But Reager was too strong. Too trained. Too cruel.

One mistake — one wrong step — and Reager grabbed him by the collar and threw him over the edge.

He fell silently into the darkness below.he died..!

Back at the structure, Alex reached out and pulled the final piece of the symbol from its resting place.

It was warm. It pulsed gently in his hand, like a heartbeat.

As he turned around, he felt something strange in the air behind him. Like a shadow pulling away.

And then he saw him — Reager, standing not too far, just outside the structure's edge.

They locked eyes.

But, Reager didn't attack.

He just stood there... smiling.

A long, twisted, creepy smile.

Then, without a word, he began to fade — dissolving like smoke into the air. But not before giving Alex one final look. Not of fear. Not of defeat.

But of satisfaction.
Like he had already done what he came to do.

Alex stared in confusion. He had no idea his best friend was gone. No idea what had been sacrificed behind him. All he knew was that something about that smile didn't feel right.

Not at all.

And then they came.

The ancient people stepped forward — silently from the shadows of the stone walls. Dozens of them. Maybe more. Their eyes locked onto him, wide with awe. Not fear. Not confusion.

Recognition.

As if they had seen him before — not him exactly, but what he represented. A prophecy. A hope. A return.

They didn't speak at first. Some fell to their knees. Others pressed a hand to their chest in silent respect. And then the elder stepped out.

His robes were worn, his face carved by time. But his voice was steady.

"You've returned," the elder said, his gaze falling on the three glowing fragments in the boy's hand. "The one who holds the pieces. The one the skies waited for."

Alex didn't speak. He just stepped forward.

The moment the three symbol pieces touched each other —
they clicked.

No force, no pressure — they just knew. And in an instant, the cracks between them vanished. A hum started. Low at first. Then rising.

A blinding beam of white light burst from the symbol and shot into the sky — cutting through the clouds like a sword. The light pulsed once... twice... then sealed.

Silent,Whole,It was done.

Gasps and cheers erupted around him. The ancient people raised their hands, shouting in a language he didn't understand — but the meaning was clear.

They were calling his name. Over and over.

The elder dropped to one knee.

"Our king has returned," he said. "The bearer of the true mark. The protector of the last dawn,

Supernova is finally here..!"

Alex looked down at the symbol now resting calmly in his palm. Solid. Unified. As if it was never meant to be apart.

He didn't feel like a king.

But in their eyes, he was everything they had waited for.

And somewhere deep inside, he felt it too.

Something had changed.

Alex was still holding the final piece. But his grip tightened.

Something was wrong, He could feel it, But he didn't know what it was, Not yet.

The Silent Goodbye

The forest felt different now. Still, but not calm. Like something was watching. Like something was... missing.

He walked slowly, not even sure why he came back this way. The ancient symbol was safe in his bag. The path forward was clear. But something inside him pulled him off-course.

Maybe it was just instinct.
Or maybe it was guilt he didn't understand yet.

A few more steps through the thick green, and something caught his eye—half-buried under a patch of leaves near the base of a twisted tree.

He stopped.
The color didn't belong. Black. Faded. Ripped.
He crouched and brushed away the leaves.
His stomach tightened.
It was a torn piece of fabric. A sleeve. The edge frayed, the cloth stained dark red.
He knew this jacket.
He had seen it a hundred times, worn by one person.
His best friend, Marc.
He didn't move. Didn't breathe.
The silence around him got heavier, like the trees were holding their breath too.

He turned the cloth over in his hand, hoping it was a mistake. Hoping it belonged to someone else. But deep down, he already knew.

The blood wasn't dry. It was recent.

His chest burned. He stood up and looked around, eyes scanning the forest for any sign—any clue that this wasn't what it looked like.

But there was nothing.

No trail. No body. Just that single, awful truth staring up from his hand.

He was here.

And now he was gone.

The weight of it crushed him. He stumbled back, hands on his head.

"No... no, no, no—"

He tried to think. Tried to make sense of it.

Why was he here? How did he even get this far?

Why didn't he say anything?

Then it hit him.

The distraction. The sound during the ambush.

The strange delay that gave him just enough time to get the last symbol.

It wasn't luck.It was him.He came here. He followed. He fought.

And he died alone.

The thought made him drop to his knees."I didn't know..." he whispered. **"I didn't even know you were here."** No one replied. Just trees. Just wind. He stayed there for a while, eyes locked on the patch of ground where the blood had dried into the soil.Then, slowly, he stood.

His face was different now. Less afraid. More focused. But harder too.The loss was real.

And now, so was the reason to finish what he started.He took one last look at the cloth, then let it fall to the earth.

"You didn't deserve this," he said quietly. "But I'll make sure it meant something."

Then he walked away.Toward the storm that was coming,The sky had cracked open with light. He was totally broken.

The symbol—finally complete—floated in his palm like it belonged to him all along. The ancient people had dropped to their knees. They had called him savior. A king. A chosen one.

But none of it mattered.

Because his best friend was stopped his breathing..!

He walked away from the stone structure in silence. No celebration. No questions. Just the dull sound of his own boots brushing against ancient dust.

The journey back was long.

He crossed the stone valley first, the place where the ancient ruins whispered with old energy. The air still buzzed faintly from the light that had shot into the sky. But now, it felt empty. Hollow. Like the symbol had taken more than it had given.

He moved through the same dense jungle, where the trees once looked magical—now just shadows and noise. Every leaf crunch felt like an echo of something lost. Every broken twig reminded him of the one person who was always behind him... now no longer.

He climbed the cliffs again—alone.

Slid down muddy slopes—alone.

Crossed the river bend.Then came the coast. The sea spread wide before him, cold and quiet.

The same sea they had crossed without knowing that Marc was following him.

He died in silence. Alone. In the shadows. While saving him.The boat rocked quietly as it cut across the waves.He didn't speak.Didn't look up. Just held the now-complete symbol close to his chest, unsure if it meant salvation or sacrifice.

He thought of the **Nyro**, the first to tell him this journey would cost him.

"You'll win... but you'll lose something that breaks you."

He didn't believe it then. He believed it now.He clenched his fists. The symbol piece was safe. The planet... maybe safe too.But his heart? It was shattered.

He was home,But not whole..

CHAPTER SIXTEEN

Before The Storm

He didn't cry. He couldn't. It was like his body refused to let anything out. But inside, everything burned.

When he finally reached the Nyro's hut — tucked between sharp cliffs and whispering trees — he didn't say a word. He just stood there, dirt-streaked and silent, with blood on his hands that wasn't his.

Nyro stepped outside, looked at him once, and saw everything.

"I know," Nyro said.

Still, Alex said nothing. He stepped forward and dropped something on the ground — a torn piece of a jacket, stained with dried blood.

That was all he needed to say.

Nyro nodded, eyes low. He picked it up, folded it gently, then walked back inside.

"You want to quit?" he asked without turning. "Tell me now."

Silence.

"I didn't think so," Nyro himself said. "Then let's begin. We don't have time."

Nyro sat down across from him and looked into his eyes.

"The cycle is almost complete. The villain will arrive soon," he said. "You've done well to get all three pieces of the symbol. But the hardest part is still ahead."

Alex's eyes didn't move. totally broken,sad,hurt,like nothingis mattered to him in this world as of now.

"You need to prepare. You will train for six months. Six months to become strong enough to fight what's coming. Nyro said silently."

Alex nodded slowly.

Nyro sighed and added, "Before that, you should see your family... and close once."

The words hit him like a stone, but his face stayed still. Inside, though, something cracked open. Nyro's voice was quiet but firm.

"This may be the last time you see them. Go. Say what needs to be said. Find strength there."

He didn't argue. He had no words. He was broken, empty.

The next day, he made the long journey back.

The town hadn't changed much. The same narrow streets, the same old trees, the same familiar faces. But to him, everything felt different — distant, fragile.

He reached his house and saw his mother at the door. Her eyes widened in disbelief, then filled with tears. She pulled him into a tight embrace. For a moment, he let himself feel the warmth. But the weight inside wouldn't lift.

His father stood silently nearby, his gaze steady but heavy. His younger sister smiled nervously, trying to act normal, but he saw the worry behind her eyes.

At dinner, words stumbled and fell. He barely spoke, but he listened. The laughter, the quiet jokes — a sharp contrast to the storm raging inside him.

Later, he found his girlfriend waiting where they always met, Lisa.— near the old bridge by the river.

She ran to him, arms wide. "You're back," she whispered.

He held her, but the distance between them was real.

"Something's wrong," she said softly, looking into his eyes.

He swallowed hard and finally spoke, voice rough.

"Marc... he didn't make it. I never got to say goodbye."

She reached up, totally shocked, instant wave of heartbreak but need to be expressive for him. touched his cheek, and said, "Then live the rest of your life like he's still watching."

For a moment, he let the pain out — silent tears falling from the eyes of both of them.

After they cry over the loss, Lisa looks him in the eye and says, *"No matter what happens... promise me you won't give up. for me, for Marc, for all of us."*

He nods, but deep down he feels the crushing weight of the path ahead — the war, the training, and the risk that he may not come back.

That night, he looked at the three pieces of the symbol, now whole and glowing faintly.

He thought of his friend, his family, and her — everything worth fighting for.

He paused outside his mother's room, watching her sleep peacefully. Her calm face struck him deeply — the same woman who had always been his strength, now unaware of the storm about to hit their lives. For a moment, he silently wished he could protect her from all this pain.

Then, he moved quietly to his little sister's room. He stepped inside and gently kissed her forehead, feeling the fragile weight of innocence resting there. A tear slipped down his cheek, and he let it fall freely for the first time in a long while. This goodbye felt heavier than anything he'd known. Without looking back, he wiped the tear away and stepped into the night, carrying the silence and sorrow with him.

At dawn, he left again.The road ahead was long...!

A Warriors Burden

Nyro's hut was quiet as the first light of dawn broke through the trees. The boy stood in front of him, still heavy with the weight of loss but determined. Nyro didn't waste words.

"The time cycle is almost complete," he said, his voice low but urgent. "**The villain, Renox will arrive soon.** You don't have much time."

The boy nodded without a word.

"To face him," Nyro continued, "you must first master your own strength. The symball's power alone won't be enough. You need to prepare your body — and your mind."

Nyro outlined the plan. "We start with physical training. Only when your body is ready will you be able to control the symball's light. It's not just a weapon, it's a force that can destroy or consume you if you're not careful."

After a moment, Nyro's expression grew serious. "You must know about the villain's power. He controls darkness — the deeper the darkness, the stronger he becomes. His strength grows as the shadows lengthen, and he can expand his reach by feeding on that darkness."

Alex clenched his fists.

"But there is a weakness,"Alex said. "Light. Pure, focused light. The power you now hold — the symball's light — can weaken him, maybe even end him."

Nyro's gaze locked with the Alex's. "But you must train. If you use the symball's power without control, it could destroy you instead. That's why we start with the trial — the physical and mental training."

Alex took a deep breath, steadying himself.

"There's no time to waste."

The morning mist clung to the trees as Alex stood before the Nyro's hut, still heavy with the weight of recent losses. The air was crisp, but inside, his chest felt like it was closing in. Nyro's gaze was steady as ever.

The main character nodded, his fingers brushing the faint glow of the symball hanging around his neck. "I'm ready."

Nyro's eyes softened for a moment. "First, you must build your body. Without strength and endurance, the power you've gained will consume you, not the other way around."

The days blurred into a relentless rhythm. The jungle became their training ground. Under the Nyro's watchful eye, Alex ran through tangled underbrush until his lungs burned, climbed jagged cliffs until his fingers were raw, and sparred with wooden weapons that bruised his arms but sharpened his reflexes.

"Faster," Nyro urged during one grueling climb. "Strength without speed is useless when darkness hunts you."

At night, by a flickering fire, Nyro spoke of the villain—the darkness incarnate.

"He thrives on shadow and fear," Nyro said, voice low, almost a whisper. "The deeper the darkness, the stronger he becomes. Light is his only weakness. But wielding that light takes more than just power."

Alex stared into the fire, the image of his best friend's face haunting him. *If only he were here...*

One evening, Nyro introduced a new trial. "Close your eyes. Face your fears."

Alone in a quiet clearing, Alex sat cross-legged, the symball resting on his palm. His mind flooded with visions — dark swirling shadows, screams, and then the face of the villain, twisted and cruel.

But then, through the shadows, came light — warm and pure. It pulsed from within him, growing stronger as he focused. The villain's darkness faltered.

Opening his eyes, he gasped. He was trembling — not just from the power, but from hope.

Yet outside, the threat grew. Nyro's hut shook one night as distant roars echoed through the valley.

"The agent is coming , Reager is coming" Nyro said grimly. "The left hand of the Renox." He hunts you relentlessly."

Alex's fists clenched. "Then I can't waste a moment."

Months had passed since that painful day, each one carving strength into Alex's soul. He had trained in silence, endured in solitude, and risen from the ashes of grief with a fire in his heart. His body was stronger, his mind sharper, and his purpose clearer than ever. The whispers of ancient energy now stirred within him—whispers of a power once thought unreachable. Maybe, just maybe, he was ready. Ready to rise as the Supernova. Ready to face Renox and bring down the dark empire that had taken everything from him...

Later, standing alone atop a hill under the stars, Alex gazed at the glowing symball.

For my best friend.

For my family.

For the world that depends on me.

A slow, fierce determination filled him. He would not fail. Not now. Not ever.

The trial was just began...

CHAPTER EIGHTEEN

Revenge Has Been Served..

The jungle was heavy and still, the kind of silence that presses down on you. Alex was deep into his training — every muscle aching, every breath heavy. Suddenly, movement flickered from the shadows. A figure stepped forward — cold, dark, familiar. The villain's agent, Reager. The same man who had taken his best friend away.

For a moment, everything stopped.

Reager :*"Well, well... look who's here. You've changed, but don't fool yourself. You're still just a boy."*

Alex :*"A boy? I'm more than that now. You took my best friend. I'm here to finish what you started."*

Reager :*"You think you can stop what's coming? You're just a spark in the endless dark."*

Alex :*"Then I'll be the fire that burns that darkness to ashes."*

Without warning, Reager lunged. But Alex was ready. Every punch, every strike was powered by months of pain, loss, and fierce determination. His fists felt like thunder, breaking through the Reager's guard, driving him back.

Blood trickled down the Reager's face, his breaths shallow and ragged.

Alex :*"You should've stayed hidden in the shadows. Now, you'll drown in the light... and your own blood."*

The light from the symball flared from his hands — sharp, bright, and unforgiving. The agent fought desperately, but his strength was fading fast.

Alex grabbed him, throwing him toward the dark river nearby. Reager screamed, splashing into the cold water.

He struggled, coughing and gasping, blood mixing with the river's flow. Alex held him tight, eyes burning with rage and grief.

Reager :"*You don't understand... the darkness never ends...*"

Alex :"*Maybe. But I'm the light that ends your darkness.*"

With a final, powerful strike, Reager went still, sinking beneath the surface. Blood spread like ink across the water, fading into the depths.

Alex stood quietly, chest heaving, staring down at the ripples. The anger inside him was heavy, but beneath it, a deep sadness settled.

Alex (softly seeing towerds sky):"*Rest now, brother. I'll carry your fight.*"

The jungle was eerily silent after the fight. Reager's body had sunk beneath the dark, flowing river, blood spreading like ink in the water. Alex stood at the edge, chest heaving, sweat and grime coating his skin. His hands trembled—not from exhaustion alone but from the storm raging inside him. He had finally taken his revenge, yet the victory felt hollow, a fragile thing that slipped through his fingers like smoke.

He stared at the fading ripples on the water's surface and whispered to himself, "I thought this would bring peace. But all I feel is emptiness." His mind flashed back to his best friend's face—the laughter they shared, the sacrifices made, the final moments stolen by Reager's cruel hand. The pain was sharp and raw, but beneath it lay a deeper question: had he truly won, or had he lost a part of himself to the darkness that fueled his rage?

Slowly, he turned away from the river, the weight of his actions pressing down on him. The fire of vengeance had burned bright, but now, standing alone beneath the heavy canopy of trees, doubt crept in like a shadow. "Is anger enough to carry me through the storm ahead?" he wondered, his voice barely audible in the thick air.

When he returned to Nyro's hut, he was waiting, his eyes steady and knowing. Without surprise, Nyro said, "You fought well today. But listen carefully—the path of revenge is a heavy one. It can blind even the strongest soul." Nyro met his gaze, voice hoarse but resolute. "I had no choice. He took everything from me. From us." Nyro nodded slowly, a sadness flickering in his eyes. "I understand. But remember, this is only the beginning. The darkness you faced was a shadow of what's coming. If you lose yourself now, there will be nothing left to fight for."

Nyro's expression darkened as he turned his gaze toward the horizon. "I sense something. The final cycle is nearing its peak. Renox is moving closer—closer than we ever imagined." A cold wind swept through the trees, rustling leaves like whispered warnings.

Alex shivered despite the heat, feeling a chill deep in his bones. This war was no longer a distant threat. It was here, looming over everything he loved and fought for. He clenched his fists, determination hardening like stone. "I won't let him take anything else," he vowed. "Not my family, not my friends, not even myself."

Nyro placed a hand on his shoulder, a rare gesture of comfort. "Then prepare yourself, for what lies ahead will test every part of you—body, mind, and soul. The true battle is about to begin."

As the night deepened, Alex stood beneath the stars, the glowing symball pulsing faintly at his chest. The light within him flickered—not just with power, but with hope, pain, and the unyielding will to protect everything worth fighting for.

He looked up at the sky, the stars faint behind the thick canopy, and whispered, **"This isn't just my fight anymore. It's for everyone I've lost... and for everyone I still have. I carry their hopes, their memories. If I fall, I want them to remember that I stood tall — not just as a warrior, but as someone who never gave up."**

Nyro's voice was soft but steady beside him: **"And that, young one, is the light that will burn the darkness away."**

Alex took a deep breath, feeling the weight of the world settle on his shoulders — but beneath it, a spark of unbreakable resolve.

Then let the darkness come. I'm ready.

CHAPTER NINETEEN

Rise Of Supernova...!

The jungle had gone quiet. No wind, no birds — just the soft crunch of leaves under Alex's boots as he walked deeper into the forest. The sun dipped low, brushing the sky with gold, casting long shadows across the moss-covered ground.

He walked slowly, hands clenched, heart strangely still.

There — the old stone.

Half-buried in the earth, covered with vines and dirt. A quiet place. A place no one else knew.

He knelt beside it, brushing off the debris gently. The initials were still there, carved with a broken knife when grief had first taken hold. His voice trembled as he spoke, barely more than a whisper.

"I did it..." he said.

"I ended him. The one who took you."

The wind didn't answer. Just a leaf tumbling to the ground.

"But it didn't bring you back."

"I thought... I thought if I could kill him, maybe the hole inside me would close. Maybe the nightmares would stop."

He paused, voice tightening.

"But now I see... it just made the shadows louder."

A tear rolled down his cheek, tracing a silent path through the dirt on his face. He didn't wipe it away.

"You were the brave one," he said, a faint smile breaking through.

"Always headfirst into chaos. And I was the one who planned

everything. The one who ran."

He swallowed.

"But now... I've stopped running. I understand what you meant when you said some things are worth fighting for."

He laid a hand on the stone, fingers trembling.

"I'm going to finish what we started. For you. For all of them. This world won't fall — not while I'm still breathing."

And then it began.

A soft hum — like a heartbeat in the air.

The symball resting on his chest began to glow — not with wild power, but with a calm, golden warmth.

It wasn't fighting him.

It was **listening**.

He closed his eyes.

That night, under the stars, he sat alone in his training yard. No weapons. No war cries. Just stillness — and the quiet presence of the symball, resting in his open palms.

His breathing slowed. His mind wandered — back to the city, the festival, the first flash of the symball, the betrayal, the battles.

But he didn't push those memories away anymore.

"I'm not the boy I was," he whispered.

"And this light... it's not a weapon. It's a memory. A promise."

Then he felt it — not heat, but **belonging**.

The symball pulsed — once. Twice.

And light poured into him.

Not bursting out, but **flowing inward**. It wrapped around his arms, climbed his chest, lit his skin in lines of radiant energy — like constellations being drawn across him.

And then...

He stood.

His clothes had changed — threads woven with energy, lightweight but unbreakable. The ancient markings of the symball etched across his chest. His eyes shimmered with starlight. His presence — calm, focused, undeniable.

He wasn't just someone holding the power anymore.

He *was* the power.

The moment was interrupted by footsteps behind him.

Nyro stepped into the clearing, silent but smiling.

"You don't need me anymore," Nyro said gently.

"My role ends here. Yours is just beginning."

He stepped closer, placing a hand on Alex's shoulder.

"Remember this — you killed the Renox's agent without your true power. Without this."

He tapped the glowing symball.

"Now, with the symball truly bonded to you... imagine what you are capable of."

Alex looked at him — eyes calm, no fear in them now. Just clarity.

He gave Nyro a small, genuine smile.

"Thank you."

Nyro nodded once — proud, quiet — then turned and walked away into the forest, vanishing into shadow like smoke.

The warrior turned to the sky..

Far away — in a fortress cloaked in endless night — Renox stirred.

His eyes flared red.He *felt* it.

The boy was gone. Something new had taken his place.

He stepped to the jagged window, clouds above twisting into unnatural spirals.

"So..." he hissed.

"He's ready."

His fingers curled.

"Then let the sky bleed."

Storms surged into being instantly. Black thunder tore through the heavens. The trees in distant lands bent and cracked. Darkness, no longer subtle, rolled across the horizon like a rising tide.

Renox's eyes narrowed.

"Light or not... I will devour him."

High on a mountaintop, where the jungle met the sky, Supernova stood alone.

The world below twisted — clouds stained red, the wind cold and sharp. The final storm had begun.

He touched the glowing emblem at his chest. The symball pulsed once, steady and sure.He took a breath.

"This isn't just my fight anymore."
"It's for those who never got a chance. For those who believed in me when I couldn't even believe in myself."

He turned to the storm.No hesitation.

"I'm ready."

And then, with fire in his veins and stars in his soul, he whispered to the wind, to the villain, to fate itself:

"I'm coming."

The sky answered with thunder. And from that moment on, he was no longer just a name in a broken story.

He was the storm's end.The world's final hope.The rise of something more.

He was Supernova..!

CHAPTER TWENTY

Before the Sky Bleeds

The clouds no longer moved like they used to. They twisted in slow, spirals — sharp edged with shadow — whispering winds that carried the scent of ash and the echo of things unsaid. Across the world, the skies had begun to bleed.

Dread had quietly settled over the lands. In far-off cities and quiet villages alike, lights flickered even when the power held. Birds flew low and never sang. Children stopped laughing. Even the animals had gone still, staring into the horizon as if they sensed something wrong waking beneath the earth.

In the southern valley, at the edge of a village slowly being devoured by creeping darkness, people huddled in silence. Mothers clutched children. Elders offered prayers to gods who had long stopped answering. Then — a whisper among them.

"He's here."

At first, it was just light — soft, golden, drifting like morning fog through the trees. Then came a hum, like a distant heartbeat. And through the forest trail, a figure emerged, glowing.

He wore no crown, no armor of legend — only a mantle of light, a calm in his stride, and a symbol pulsing steadily at his chest. He wasn't the boy who had once fled battle and wept at graves.

He was Supernova.

No fanfare. No army. Just presence. He stepped forward, quiet and unshaken, into the heart of the village where thick shadow-creatures hissed and writhed through alleyways, fusing with the walls, spitting black smoke into the air. People backed away in fear.

But Supernova didn't strike. He didn't raise a weapon.

He stepped into the center square, slowly dropped to one knee, and closed his eyes. He breathed.

The symball on his chest flared with gentle gold. A soundless pulse rippled outward from him like the exhale of the earth itself. It washed over the square, over the creatures — and they began to vanish. Not shattered. Not destroyed. Just... unmade. Like fog touched by sunlight.

The people of town stared, wide-eyed, as the last of the darkness hissed and withered away. For the first time in days, the air felt breathable again.

Supernova rose.

"You're safe now," he said softly, turning to go.

"Wait!" one of the elders called, her voice trembling. "What do we call you, light bearer?"

He paused, then turned back to her.

"Supernova."

And with that one word, hope was reborn.

The wind changed again — this time not warm, but sharp. Humens looked up.

The clouds were twisting unnaturally, and then — with a sound like thunder tearing through silk — a rift split the sky. A jagged wound opened across the heavens, and through it, he came.

The villain's face appeared — vast, hollow-eyed, and built of shadow. His voice boomed across the lands, a curse etched in air. Arrival of Renox..

"Three moonrises," he said, his voice echoing through every ear. "That is all the time you have left."

A hush fell over the village.

"The bleed cannot be stopped now. The final eclipse will mark the end — of time, of light, of mercy."

Then, his gaze — even from the sky — locked with Supernova's.

"You've glowed long enough," he whispered, darker now, colder. "Let's see how bright you burn when the sky falls."

And then the sky sealed shut again. The rift vanished. Only thunder remained.

Supernova stood still, fists slowly curling. There was no fear in his eyes. Only fire.

That night, he returned to the summit — the sacred mountaintop where light first found him. Alone, he unrolled the ancient symball scrolls, pages once sealed, now alight with energy.

Visions poured into him — not dreams, but memories. Not his.

The villain's.

Once, he too had borne the light. Once, he was a protector.

But somewhere, he broke. A loss, a betrayal, or perhaps a crack too small to notice until it swallowed him whole. He hadn't been consumed. He had surrendered.

Supernova saw what could've been his future — if he had clung to revenge, if he had fed his rage instead of letting it go at the grave. They were mirrors. But only one of them had chosen to burn without purpose.

Then came the final truth.

The Bleed — it wasn't the end. It was a test.

Light was never forged to destroy darkness.

It was created to balance it. To confront. To heal. And only if all else failed — to seal it away.

He stood, wind pulling at his cloak, and called his allies back from exile. Fighters, seers, the forgotten ones who still believed in light. They came, gathering around him like sparks drawn to flame.

"This isn't just about survival," Supernova told them. "It's about meaning. About who we choose to be when the last choice is given."

"For the world we want to leave behind."

Someone asked him, "And if we fail?"

Supernova looked up. His symball glowed bright at his chest.

"Then we burn so bright the stars remember."

When the gathering had ended, when the night had fallen, and only the stars remained, Supernova opened the final page of the scroll.

One line burned into him.

When the sky bleeds, the soul decides.

He looked out across the horizon, where red clouds now loomed.

"Let it bleed," he whispered.

"I'm ready."

Thunder cracked above.

And somewhere far below, the last moonrise began.

CHAPTER TWENTY-ONE

The End Game..!

The sky looked wrong.

It wasn't just red—it was bleeding. Dark clouds spun like a whirlpool above the battlefield, casting a sick glow over the land. Nothing moved. No birds, no wind. Just a broken world waiting for its final blow.

And in the middle of it, he walked—alone.

Supernova.

His boots hit the dry, cracked earth one step at a time. The air felt heavy. But his heart was calm. No more running. No more fear. This was it.

Across the field, Renox stepped out from the mist. Tall, cold, eyes glowing with darkness. His black coat dragged behind him like a shadow.

"You finally showed up," Renox said, almost amused.

Supernova stopped, a few feet away. "You already knew I would."

Renox tilted his head. "You look different. Stronger. But also... tired."

Supernova's voice was steady. "I've lost people. I've carried guilt. I've bled for this moment. Of course I'm tired."

Renox smiled cruelly. "Well, let's end your pain."

And just like that, he attacked.

A wave of shadow came crashing forward, like a tidal wave made of smoke and claws. Supernova raised his arms, and a shield of glowing light expanded around him. The shadows slammed into it with a deafening boom—but didn't break through.

The battle began.

They clashed in the middle, fist to fist, power against power. Light against shadow. No tricks. No backup. Just two forces trying to break the other.

"You think you've changed!" Renox shouted, swinging a blade of pure darkness. "You're still that scared boy looking for a reason to fight!"

Supernova blocked the blade with a wall of light and shoved him back. "I'm not scared anymore."

Their powers lit up the sky—white and black bolts tearing through trees, splitting the ground, shaking the clouds above.

Blow after blow.

Kick, dodge, slam—neither backing down.

"You'll lose!" Renox yelled. "You're fighting alone!"

Supernova's eyes narrowed. "No. I'm fighting with everything I've become."

Renox roared and tackled him. They crashed through a wall of stone. Supernova rolled, coughed blood, stood up again.

"You're still standing?" Renox gasped, shocked.

"Barely," Supernova said, wiping his mouth. "But enough."

They ran at each other again. This time, there was no holding back. Every ounce of power. Every scream. Every tear. The ground turned to fire beneath them.

And finally, Renox slammed Supernova down hard.

He hit the dirt. Couldn't move.

Chest rising and falling. Pain everywhere. Eyes blurry.

Renox stood over him, laughing. *I warned you. Hope is weak. Light dies.*

Supernova didn't answer.

Instead, he reached for his chest—where the symball glowed softly.

His voice was quiet, but strong.

"You were wrong."

The symball flared.

"I didn't need the light to kill your agent, Reager."

The villain stepped back, confused.

"I didn't need it to survive the pain."

Supernova slowly got to his knees.

"I needed it to remember who I am."

Then—he stood.

And the symball burst into golden fire.

A beam of pure light rose from his body, swirling with energy. Renox raised his hands in defense.

"What—what is this?!"

Supernova's voice shook the air.

"This is what happens when you fight for more than yourself."

The ground cracked. Light wrapped around his arms and chest. His eyes turned white.

"You tried to end the world."

He pointed both palms at the Renox.

"I'm ending you."

He screamed, and the beam fired—huge, unstoppable, a storm of light that tore through the air and slammed into Renox with explosive force.

Renox screamed.

Light consumed him.

And then... silence.

Nothing but dust.

Supernova dropped to the ground. Gasping. Bloodied. Barely breathing.

He had done it. He was alive. Just barely. He lay there, staring at the clouds. The sky was turning blue again. The red was fading. The storm was ending. Then... he saw him, Nyro. Nyro was there.

Standing behind a tree, watching. Silent.Thcy locked eyes.Nyro smiled—proud, gentle.

Supernova smiled back, weak but full of peace.And in that moment...Nyrohe Old Man vanished,Gone.

Supernova closed his eyes.The war was over.The world had been saved.And as the wind picked up, carrying away the last ashes of darkness, Supernova whispered one final line...

"The light didn't save me. I became the light."

One month later...

The world was quiet. No chaos. No alarms. Just the soft hum of life returning to normal. Birds chirped outside the window. Morning sunlight filtered gently through the curtains. Alex stood alone in his apartment — no noise, no company, just the echo of a silence that now felt permanent. He poured himself a cup of coffee, the old habit grounding him. The warmth in his hands was real. So was the weight in his chest. He stepped out onto the balcony. The sky was golden — the kind of light that used to mean hope. Down below, the city moved like nothing had changed. People laughed. Cars passed. Life went on. And maybe for most people, it hadn't changed at all. But he knew. He remembered every scar, every sacrifice, every impossible choice. And he remembered Marc — the laughs they shared, the fights they barely survived, the brotherhood that no battle could ever break. Except the last one.

"Marc had always said we'd make it out together. But the war had different plans."

Alex had saved the galaxy... but not his best friend. He looked up at the horizon, blinking away the sting in his eyes.

"I kept my promise. We finished what we started."

There was no reply. Just the wind, and the soft rustle of leaves. He stood there a moment longer, letting the silence hold him. The hero. The survivor. The one left behind. Then, with a quiet breath and the ghost of a smile, he raised his cup to the sky — to Marc, to what they lost, and to what they saved.

"The galaxy can rest for now. And maybe, just maybe — so can I."